COULD YOU SURVIVE THE NEW STONE AGE?

AN INTERACTIVE PREHISTORIC ADVENTURE

BY THOMAS KINGSLEY TROUPE
ILLUSTRATED BY JUAN CALLE

Content Consultant: Mathew Wedel, PhD
Associate Professor, Department of Anatomy
Western University of Health Sciences
Pomona, California

CAPSTONE PRESS
a capstone imprint

You Choose Books are published by Capstone Press, an imprint of Capstone.
1710 Roe Crest Drive
North Mankato, Minnesota 56003
www.capstonepub.com

Library of Congress Cataloging-in-Publication Data:
Names: Troupe, Thomas Kingsley, author. | Calle, Juan, 1977- illustrator.
Title: Could you survive the New Stone Age? : an interactive prehistoric
adventure / by Thomas Kingsley Troupe ; illustrated by Juan Calle. Description:
North Mankato, Minnesota : Capstone Press, [2020] | Series: You choose:
prehistoric survival | Includes bibliographical references and index. | Audience:
Ages 8-11. | Audience: Grades 4-6. | Summary: The reader's choices determine
whether three friends will survive after being mysteriously transported back in time
to the Neolithic Era, when humans were first learning to farm and harvest and to
domesticate animals. Identifiers: LCCN 2019045012 (print) | LCCN 2019045013
(ebook) | ISBN 9781543574050 (hardcover) | ISBN 9781496658104 (paperback)
| ISBN 9781543574098 (pdf) Subjects: LCSH: Plot-your-own stories. | CYAC:
Prehistoric peoples--Fiction. | Prehistoric animals--Fiction. | Time travel--Fiction.
| Paleontology--Fiction. | Adventure and adventurers--Fiction. | Plot-your-own
stories. Classification: LCC PZ7.D692 Cou 2020 (print) | LCC PZ7.D692 (ebook)
| DDC [Fic]--dc23 LC record available at https://lccn.loc.gov/2019045012 LC
ebook record available at https://lccn.loc.gov/2019045013

Summary: Leads readers through a New Stone Age adventure in which they can
choose what to do and where to go next.

Design Elements
Capstone and Shutterstock: Eucalyp

Editorial Credits
Editor: Mandy Robbins; Designer: Bobbie Nyutten; Media Researcher: Jo Miller;
Production Specialist: Tori Abraham

All internet sites appearing in back matter were available and accurate when this
book was sent to press.

Printed and bound in the USA.
3163

TABLE OF CONTENTS

TRAPPED IN THE PAST

YOU are an ordinary kid going about your everyday life. Suddenly, you find yourself in a strange place and a strange time. It's a period from long ago. The world looks different than anything you've ever seen before. Terrifying beasts roam the land. Danger lurks at every turn. Where will you find shelter? How will you get food? Will you ever see your friends and family again? Most importantly of all, can you survive?

Chapter One sets the scene. Then you choose which path to take. Follow the directions at the bottom of each page. The choices you make determine what happens next. After you finish your path, go back and read the others for more adventures.

YOU CHOOSE the path you take through the New Stone Age!

Turn the page to begin your adventure.

5

CHAPTER ONE
FANTASTIC FIELD TRIP

Your middle school class is on a field trip at the National Museum of Ancient Studies with your history teacher, Mr. Hassan. He leads you through a darkened doorway as the tour guide ushers your class from the last exhibit into the new one. A banner reading, "Welcome to the New Stone Age," hangs above the walkway.

Life-sized dioramas show people during the New Stone Age. Mannequins dressed in animal skins and furs are in an ancient farm scene. Their motionless hands hold handmade tools.

"Creepy," your friend Jorge says.

"Yeah," you reply. "They almost look real."

You turn your attention to the tour guide.

Turn the page.

"The New Stone Age, or Neolithic, changed the world's history," she explains. "People back then learned to farm and harvest their food instead of only hunting in the wild."

"Good," Mishil whispers. "Give the animals a break."

The tour guide smiles.

"Animals played an important part in Neolithic times," she says, pointing to another display. "People learned to domesticate and raise them on their farms. Dogs became companions while cattle, sheep, and other animals provided milk and food."

Mr. Hassan told everyone to stay together, but you, Jorge, and Mishil are dawdling at a nearby display. It shows people making tools. The mannequins appear to sharpen stones to make axes and handheld tools for farming called adzes.

Behind them, a scene shows mannequins posed to look like they're building small square structures. Ladders lean against the walls.

"So, where are the dinosaurs?" Jorge asks.

Mishil laughs. "Dinosaurs were long gone before the Neolithic Era began," she says.

After making jokes about the Stone Age haircuts, you spot a knife made with a shiny, black stone blade. It's just inside the display ropes and it seems to pull you in. You can't help yourself. You have to touch it. Out of the corners of your eyes, you see Jorge and Mishil reach to touch the blade too.

In a blinding flash, the museum is gone. You're suddenly in the middle of a hilly countryside. The air is fresher than any you've ever breathed.

Turn the page.

Behind you are Jorge and Mishil. You are all dressed in animal skins. Somehow you've all jumped back more than 7,000 years in time.

"This is some field trip," you whisper.

"So," Jorge asks. "How do we get back?"

"I'm not sure we can," Mishil says. "I think we're trapped in the past!"

In shock, you walk across the tall grass to look out over the valley. There's a small farm in the distance. You can't tell if people are there, but a thin tendril of smoke rises to the sky.

"Hey," Jorge says. "I think there's a village way out there."

You turn and look to where he's pointing. Whatever is out there is partially hidden by the hill, but there are even more lines of smoke rising into the sky. More fires means more people, right?

"Maybe we can live at that farm for a while," you say.

"I don't know," Jorge admits. "Farming sounds like hard work."

"Or we head for that village out there," you suggest. "Maybe we can live there."

"That's a long walk from here," Mishil says, looking over the valley.

Jorge pauses to survey the land.

"We could hunt and gather," Jorge says. "You know, live off the land like nomads."

None of the choices seem great. But to survive, you'll have to make one.

To head to the nearby farm, turn the page.
To find the great village of Çatalhöyük, turn to page 43.
To try to live like a nomad in the wilderness, turn to page 71.

CHAPTER TWO

ON THE FARM

The farm seems like the best place to find food. The three of you set off in that direction. You walk for an hour as the sun warms your skin. All around you are grassy fields and rolling hills. In the far distance, you see mountains.

"Listen," Mishil says. "No cars, no airplanes."

Soon you reach the edge of the farm. There are two small wooden huts with grass roofs. Some odd-looking cows graze in a nearby field.

You see at least 15 people on the farm. Some are working in the field, using primitive tools to dig into the dirt. Others are pulling crops from the soil. The farmers are dressed in animal skins and rough fabrics.

Turn the page.

One of the women sees you and shouts something you don't understand. The others in the field look up.

A strong-looking man with a serious face walks your way. Two men with spears appear at his side. They look ready to attack.

"I don't like this," Jorge mutters.

"They don't either," you reply.

"We have to show them we mean no harm," Mishil replies. "But how?"

To show you have nothing in your hands,
go to the next page.

To touch your stomachs and point to their crops,
turn to page 18.

Your heart pounds as you step forward. You raise your hands up and hold them open.

"Please help," you say, sure they won't understand. "We are lost and hungry."

The big man's face softens and he touches the spears. His men lower them. You exhale in relief. You suspect they don't always get friendly visitors appearing from nowhere.

A middle-aged couple takes you into a hut. The woman feeds you beans on a clay plate and milk in a handmade cup. The farmers quickly realize you are no threat. You and your friends sleep that night on a small patch of straw in one of the shelters.

As the weeks go on, you become like a part of the family, even picking up some of their language.

Turn the page.

The farmers show you how to farm and how to know if the crops are ripe. Wheat, for instance, falls to the ground when it's ripe. The farmers show you how to till the ground with a tool that looks like an axe.

"That's an adze," Mishil says with a smirk. "I paid attention to the tour guide."

After a long day of work a woman offers you some bread she's baked in a small stone oven. The other Stone Age people are eating their bread and drinking from handmade clay cups.

Your stomach growls as you stuff the bread into your mouth. It's warm but tastes bitter.

"It's gross," Jorge whispers with a frown.

You agree.

To ask for something else to eat, turn to page 21.
To finish eating the bread and pretend that you like it, turn to page 22.

"They need to know we're hungry and want to learn how to farm," you tell your classmates.

You point to the crops and then to your stomach. Almost immediately the big farmer's face grows stern. The two men with spears advance as if angry with you. The big man does nothing to stop them. Other farmers raise fists into the air as if urging the guardians on.

"Maybe not the best idea," Mishil gasps. "They think we wanted to steal their food."

She puts her hands up as if in surrender. Seeing this, you and Jorge do the same. Your actions spur the farm guardians to stop and look back at their leader. He nods, and they lower their spears.

Mishil whispers, "We have to be careful how we communicate with them."

The farmers are watching your group suspiciously. You try a different hand gesture, pointing to your mouth as if showing you would like to eat. Almost immediately, a woman from the field brings you a handful of dried beans. They don't look tasty, but you all take some and eat them.

"I wish we could've cooked them first," Jorge says after gulping down his beans.

You're no longer considered thieves looking to steal from them. The farmers take your group in and put you to work. In the following weeks you learn to till fields, plant seeds, and harvest crops.

One night, while everyone else is asleep, you wake up. Your stomach is growling with hunger. You haven't been eating as much as you usually do, and you know it's because you're still not used to the food in Neolithic times.

Turn the page.

Whenever this happened back in your own time, you'd head down to the kitchen for a snack. Even though you've been made to feel welcome on the farm, you're still a bit of an outsider. You wonder if it's a good idea to take some of the food the farmers have collected.

To sneak out and find something to eat, turn to page 40.
To tough it out and wait until morning, turn to page 41.

The bread tastes terrible. You can't hide your disgust, so you use the few words you know to ask for some other food. They seem offended you don't like the bread.

"They're not happy with you," Mishil says.

She smiles, pretending to like the bread. Jorge does the same.

The woman snatches the remains of your bread. No one offers you anything else to eat for the rest of the day. As you work in the fields later on, you wish you'd been grateful for the bread.

When you finally lie down, you can't sleep because you're so hungry. Maybe you should get up and find something to eat on your own. There's more than enough food for everyone.

To look for something to eat, turn to page 40.
To ignore your stomach and wait until morning, turn to page 41.

Though difficult, you pretend the bread is delicious. The farmers seem satisfied. As they return to work, you gather your friends.

"If we want to keep living here, we have to pitch in and help out," you say.

"Yes," Mishil says. "Otherwise we're just extra mouths to feed."

You watch a group of men carrying handmade tools that look like shovels. The tools have wide, flat stones attached to longer sticks with rough cords. The group moves through a dry field where small plants are sprouting. Thinking it might be a great opportunity to help them, you each pick up a nearby shovel and follow them into the field.

The farmers begin digging a small trench near the crops. Nearby you hear a creek bubbling.

Turn the page.

"They're digging irrigation trenches," Mishil whispers. "That's how they bring water to dry parts of their fields."

"Let's help them out," Jorge says.

Since they're working closer to the field, you climb a small hill near the stream. The farmers seem to be routing the trenches around the hill. You think making a trench that runs downhill would save time. Digging a trench all the way around will take longer.

To dig a trench in the hill, go to the next page.
To follow the path the farmers are digging, turn to page 28.

To save time and energy, you decide to dig a channel from the stream and down the hill. The farmers continue working around the hill, but you think they will prefer your way when you're done.

Your team digs into the dirt. Before long, water fills the channel you created. You shovel the path to the top of the hill and your friends widen it along the way.

You look to see how the other farmers are doing, but can't see them from your position on the hill. In minutes, they'll cheer when they see how much easier your way is.

As you dig further into the hill, water rushes down the slope. Suddenly you realize your mistake. The water is flowing toward the newly budded crops. You watch as water washes out the small plants and floods the field, quickly turning it from dry soil to sopping mud.

Turn the page.

The farmers suddenly realize what you've done. They're furious that you've flooded their crops.

"I don't think we're welcome here anymore," Mishil says.

You and your friends run away from the farm. Night falls quickly. You wander for a while until you come upon a thicket of trees. Exhausted, you and your friends collapse for the night.

"We can figure out what to do in the morning," Mishil says. "Let's rest now."

But morning never comes for you. At some point in the night you awaken to a rumbling growl. You blink awake to see an enormous lion ready to pounce. You don't even have time to scream as its giant paws slam into your head.

THE END

To follow another path, turn to page 11.
To learn more about the New Stone Age, turn to page 103.

"Let's do it their way," you suggest. "They must know what they're doing."

You help dig a narrow trench that winds past the hill and to the stream. One of the farmers digs smaller trenches between the sprouts.

After several hours, the trenches are done. A farmer lifts a rock he'd set in front of the inlet, and water fills the grooves in the field. When the water overflows and reaches the plants, one of the farmers calls to block it up again.

You're impressed by their system of watering crops. The farmers pick up their tools and motion for you to follow them.

They lead you to a field where nine cows graze. The cows are different from what you're used to. They each have large, curved horns, dark skin, and a white stripe down their backs.

"Those are aurochs—ancient cows," Mishil whispers.

The sour tang of manure hits your nose, making your eyes water. The farmers shovel the manure from around the cows. They dump it onto a filthy animal skin stretched over two thick, wooden sticks. When they have a decent load, they drag the stretcher of manure to the field of crops.

"So here's our new chore," Mishil says.

You and your friends shovel up most of the piles the aurochs have left behind. You don't know how to handle these ancient cows, so you decide to work around them. There are a few piles of manure left beneath where the animals are standing, but the work is mostly done. The farmers don't seem to mind.

Turn the page.

"I'm wiped," Mishil says. "I hope we can rest for a while."

You agree, but your workday isn't over yet. Farm life in the Neolithic is hard work. The farmers have you pull beans from the field, dig planting rows, and feed the animals. You get a break and are given a little water to drink from a clay cup. Your friends look miserable. You've never been this sore.

"I'm done working for the day," Jorge decides. "I'm going to collapse."

"I'm tired too, but we can't stop working. What if they throw us off the farm?" Mishil asks.

To stop working until tomorrow, turn the page.
To keep doing what the farmers ask, turn to page 34.

You just can't work any longer. You toss down your tools and approach the farm's leader. With hand gestures you show him that you and your friends are done for the day.

The man's eyes narrow. He leads you and your friends away from the rest of the workers.

"Perfect," Jorge says. "He's okay with us taking a rest! Maybe he'll feed us too."

At the edge of the farm the man points out to the hills where the sun is setting.

"No, no," you say. "We just don't want to work anymore today."

The man points again to the hills.

"We're being thrown out," Mishil says. "If we can't work like the rest of the community, they have no use for us."

The three of you walk away from the farm, tired, hungry, and upset. You press on into the dusk, finding it harder to see as time wears on. As you approach an open stretch between clusters of snarled trees, you see a freshly killed caribou carcass. You imagine how good it will taste roasted over a fire and take a few excited steps forward.

"Wait!" Mishil shouts. "It's a trapping pit!"

They're the last words you hear.

You fall through a thin layer of thatched grass and into a pit of spikes. Some hunters must have dug it to trap and kill animals. The spikes pierce your body, and you quickly bleed to death.

THE END

To follow another path, turn to page 11.
To learn more about the New Stone Age, turn to page 103.

Even though you're worn out, you can't let everyone else on the farm do all the work. It's not fair.

Your friends are ready to collapse, but they agree. Farm work is hard, but maybe in time you'll get used to it. You continue the work assigned to you, grateful these ancient farmers have taken you in.

You work in the fields until the sun starts to set. Then a man hands you a spear. You're not sure what to do.

"Am I supposed to fight him?" you ask Mishil.

The man touches his eyes and points to the hills.

"I think you two are on guard duty," Mishil says. "You have to watch for attackers. The tour guide said nomads would steal from farmers."

You and the man stand guard. As evening approaches, you spot a large group of men farther down the hill. They're armed with bows and axes. Your partner exclaims something that you don't understand. He's giving you an order, but you don't know what it is. Your grip tightens around the spear as you wonder what to do.

To attack the approaching nomads and defend the farm, turn the page.

To warn the farmers about the nomads, turn to page 37.

You take a deep breath. Your think your job is to defend the farm. As the men get closer, you run toward them, spear raised for attack. Your partner cries out and launches his spear before you get a chance to throw yours.

The spear strikes one of the nomads in the leg. He drops, screeching in pain. The others roar in anger and run toward the farm. You throw your own spear, but it sails over their heads.

The sound of bowstrings firing fills the air. Two arrows hit you in the chest with red-hot stings. You fall to the ground. The last things you hear are nomads shouting and trampling past you as the farm is raided.

THE END

To follow another path, turn to page 11.
To learn more about the New Stone Age, turn to page 103.

With zero combat experience, you know you won't get anywhere near the nomads before you're killed. Besides, they outnumber you 11 to two.

The guard must be telling you to run for help. You scramble to warn the other farmers. At least 20 of them grab their weapons and run your way.

The farm's leader shouts, and the nomads stop in their tracks. The sight of the armed farmers is enough for the nomads to back off. They disappear into the hills as if knowing they stood no chance.

The group is relieved to have stopped an attack. You are rewarded for helping keep the nomads at bay with a meal of meat and beans. You begin to think that maybe farm life isn't so bad.

You huddle with your friends near the fire. Then you spy a familiar, black-bladed knife on the ground.

"Hey," you whisper. "Do you see this?"

Turn the page.

Both Mishil and Jorge look down at the familiar weapon.

"It's the knife from the museum," Jorge says.

"Yeah," Mishil agrees. "That's what got us here in the first place."

The three of you reach for the stone, and in a flash—you're back in the museum.

"Keep up," Mr. Hassan says from the front of the group. "We don't want to lose anyone."

"Will do," Jorge says, then turns to you. "And remember—don't touch anything!"

You smile and stuff your hands in the front pockets of your jeans.

"No problem," you say.

THE END

To follow another path, turn to page 11.
To learn more about the New Stone Age, turn to page 103.

You just can't deal with the hunger. You have to find something to eat. Being careful not to wake anyone else, you carefully step out of the small hut and into the night. Other than the moon and the stars, there is no light.

The field is close, and you decide to just pick some peas for a quick midnight snack. You sneak through the crops to an area the farmers were hoping to harvest tomorrow. You pop a pea pod into your mouth.

Behind you a stick snaps. You turn to see someone approaching. You forgot about the night guards! They probably don't recognize you in the dark. Before you can say anything, you feel a spear pierce your stomach. Your time in the New Stone Age is over.

THE END

To follow another path, turn to page 11.
To learn more about the New Stone Age, turn to page 103.

You awake the next morning, hungrier than ever. You're thankful for your bowl of mashed lentils and water. It's not the breakfast you prefer, but it beats going hungry.

As the days and weeks go by, you settle into the routine of hard work on the farm. You learn some of the language and make friends in the community. You even develop a taste for the Stone Age bread. You still miss your home, but you, Jorge, and Mishil have carved out a nice life together on the farm. Until you can find your way back to modern times, you're happy to stay here.

THE END

To follow another path, turn to page 11.
To learn more about the New Stone Age, turn to page 103.

CHAPTER THREE

GREAT VILLAGE

The village would have more people, which means more help for you and your friends. You head toward the smoke rising into the air.

"It looks like the great village of Çatalhöyük," Mishil says. "We're in Turkey."

"It's pretty big," Jorge says.

"For its time, it is," Mishil says. "There were around 8,000 people living here at one point."

As you get closer, you see hundreds of rectangular homes clustered together. A few have tiny windows. Each home has a square entrance in the roof, accessed by a ladder. Soon you reach the edge of the village. Villagers watch you approach from a distance. They seem suspicious of you.

Turn the page.

"They don't look happy to see us," Jorge whispers.

The village is busy. Some people tend crops in fields in the distance. Another group is digging in the ground, pulling chunks of mud from the soil. Still others are building more shelters for people to live in. Another group works on making tools and weapons. Spears and knives lie on the ground nearby.

"We should grab one of those," Jorge says, nodding to the knives. "Just in case."

He might be right. You might need a weapon if you have to defend yourself. And if they don't take you in, a knife would help for hunting and survival.

"No, we should talk to the people," Mishil says. "Stealing isn't a great first impression."

To stop Jorge from stealing a knife, go to the next page.
To tell Jorge to sneak a knife while you talk to the villagers, turn to page 47.

"Leave the knives alone," you say. "Let's see if these people are friendly. Taking something will only make them mad."

"You're probably right," Jorge replies.

Mishil gestures to the villagers, mimicking the work they are doing, then points to herself and the rest of your group. A woman with long scraggly hair and deep creases in her face nods. She waves for you to follow her.

"Now we're getting somewhere," you say.

Jorge still looks worried. "I hope it's not somewhere they can kill us," he whispers.

You walk toward the houses inside the village. The woman stops and gestures to two different dwellings. One of them is complete but appears abandoned. The other is being worked on by two villagers.

Turn the page.

"I think they're asking us where we'd like to stay," Mishil says.

You look at the existing hut. After your long trek across the plains, it would be great to relax and figure out what to do next. The men working on the new hut are sweating in the sun, shaping the mud and plaster along the new structure. It looks like hard work. Maybe you should choose that one and offer to help.

To take the existing hut, turn to page 57.
To help the others build a new hut, turn to page 58.

"Grab a knife," you whisper. "But be careful. If they see you take it, we're going to have trouble."

Jorge nods. You and Mishil walk toward the villagers, hoping to block Jorge. Mishil walks ahead with her hands out to show you mean no harm.

"We are lost. Can you help us?" she asks.

The villagers can't understand anything she's saying. They actually look a little more suspicious.

"Maybe we should forget this," you whisper.

You glance over your shoulder. Jorge stands up and walks over to the two of you. If he managed to grab the knife no one seemed to notice.

Instead of words, Mishil tries something else. She gestures to you and Jorge and nods to the city. An older man with a large scar on his face steps forward. He says something in a strange language and gestures for you to come closer.

Turn the page.

"It worked," you whisper.

As the three of you advance, something falls to the ground. It strikes a stone, making a loud sound. You don't even have to look to see what it is. The knife has fallen from wherever Jorge stowed it. The welcoming face of the village leader turns angry.

"We're busted," Jorge says. "We should run!"

"No, no," Mishil says. "We give it back to them and apologize!"

That might be the right thing to do, but you aren't sure they'll understand or trust you anymore. Running might be your best chance to survive.

To give the knife back, turn the page.
To keep the knife and run for your lives, turn to page 52.

"Give it back!" you shout to Jorge.

As the villagers advance, Jorge holds the knife out with both hands. He looks at it with fascination and touches the handle and rough stone blade. He's showing appreciation for the weapon's craftsmanship. He's hoping to appeal to their pride. It works.

A big man steps forward and takes the blade. He calls over a short, muscular man with black soot on his cheeks. The man looks at the knife and then taps his chest once.

"He made that knife," you whisper.

The knife-maker looks up and points to you and then to the knife. He points to a small workspace near one of the square dwellings.

"I think he wants to show us how he made it," Mishil says.

"Give it back!" you shout to Jorge.

As the villagers advance, Jorge holds the knife out with both hands. He looks at it with fascination and touches the handle and rough stone blade. He's showing appreciation for the weapon's craftsmanship. He's hoping to appeal to their pride. It works.

A big man steps forward and takes the blade. He calls over a short, muscular man with black soot on his cheeks. The man looks at the knife and then taps his chest once.

"He made that knife," you whisper.

The knife-maker looks up and points to you and then to the knife. He points to a small workspace near one of the square dwellings.

"I think he wants to show us how he made it," Mishil says.

"It worked," you whisper.

As the three of you advance, something falls to the ground. It strikes a stone, making a loud sound. You don't even have to look to see what it is. The knife has fallen from wherever Jorge stowed it. The welcoming face of the village leader turns angry.

"We're busted," Jorge says. "We should run!"

"No, no," Mishil says. "We give it back to them and apologize!"

That might be the right thing to do, but you aren't sure they'll understand or trust you anymore. Running might be your best chance to survive.

To give the knife back, turn the page.
To keep the knife and run for your lives, turn to page 52.

"Or he wants to stab us for taking his knife?" Jorge says.

The village leader leans over and picks up a large ceramic jar from the ground. It was set against the wall of another home. He shows it to you and your friends proudly.

"It's nice," you say, nodding toward it.

"I think he's offering to teach us to make pottery too. Doing some work might be our chance to show we can be useful to their community."

Pottery seems like the easier option. Crafting knives and spears will definitely be more work. But it might be more interesting.

To learn to make pottery, turn to page 63.
To learn how to make knives, turn to page 54.

There's no going back from stealing a knife from a village of New Stone Agers. There's only one thing to do.

"Run!" you shout.

The three of you turn and sprint away from the village. You hear angry footsteps thundering after you.

"There's nowhere to hide!" Mishil cries.

Way off in the distance, you see mountains, but know there's no way you'll ever reach them.

A spear whistles past your head and sticks up from the ground. You grab it, hoping it will be enough to defend yourselves.

To your left, Mishil drops to the ground, an arrow sticking out of her back. Jorge is struggling to catch up with you. A moment later, he cries out. He goes down too.

Your legs are burning, and your lungs feel like they're on fire. You were already exhausted when you reached the city. Why did you tell Jorge to steal that knife? Your legs buckle, and you fall. In seconds, there are more than 10 angry men standing above you. One of them raises a spear and drives it into you. The world goes black.

THE END

To follow another path, turn to page 11.
To learn more about the New Stone Age, turn to page 103.

You decide to follow the knife-maker. Maybe you can learn how to make knives and spears.

"This way if we get tossed out of the village, we can make our own weapons out in the wild," Jorge says.

"Let's hope that doesn't happen," Mishil says.

You walk toward the house with the shorter villager, and he shows you the pile of flat stones he's collected. He takes one and grinds it against a large stone that is covered with scrape marks. The man works one end and then another. In time he shapes the stone into something that resembles a blade.

He shows you how to shape wood into a handle and attach it to the blade with cord. Then he lets you try it. You struggle while Mishil and Jorge seem to pick up the skill with ease.

Turn the page.

In the following weeks, you get better at your craft. During that time, you're given a home and are well fed. You've earned the trust of the community and work hard every day. You truly feel like you're part of the village, even learning enough of their language to get by.

You still miss home, but you've made a life for yourself here. Until you can find a way back, you're content making New Stone Age tools and weapons.

THE END

To follow another path, turn to page 11.
To learn more about the New Stone Age, turn to page 103.

"Let's take the one that's already built," you say and point to the older hut. The woman smiles as if welcoming you to your new home.

You climb the ladder and enter the hut from the hole in the roof. As soon as you descend into the shady room, a disgusting stink rises from somewhere inside. You've been near other huts in the village, but they didn't smell like this. It's like rotten meat and vomit.

"It smells nasty!" Jorge cries.

You're not sure you can live here. Your stomach turns with every passing moment.

"We can't refuse this place now," Mishil says. "It would be insulting."

To refuse the hut, turn to page 60.
To stick it out in the stinky hut, turn to page 61.

Something feels wrong about taking an existing hut while others build a new one.

"Let's show them we're willing to work," you say.

You point to the hut builders. The woman seems pleased. The three of you work with the others. You haul wet mud to the site and help shape the walls with flat rocks.

You spend the next few weeks building more homes. You even learn a few primitive words. The village elder appreciates your help. When the homes are complete, he asks if you would like to make pottery or care for the animals.

"Pottery seems easy enough," Mishil says. "I'll do that."

"I'd rather take care of animals," Jorge says.

To learn to craft pottery with Mishil, turn to page 63.
To go with Jorge to care for the animals, turn to page 64.

"I can't do this," you say with a gag.

You climb out of the house and find the old woman looking through some of the grain and beans collected from the fields. She sees you plugging your nose and pointing to the hut. The woman's face turns angry. She points out toward the great wide open. She's ordering you and your friends to leave.

The three of you walk away from the village. You can't remember how to get back to the farm you saw when you first arrived in the past, and night is falling.

You're not sure what to do. The three of you sleep in an open field that night. You wander the grasslands for weeks with no luck finding consistent food or shelter. In less than a month you're too weak to go on. Starving and weary, you and your friends die.

THE END

To follow another path, turn to page 11.
To learn more about the New Stone Age, turn to page 103.

"We need to make the best of this," you say.

You stuff wet leaves into your nostrils to help block the stink. Jorge seems driven to figure out the smell's source. He squats and brushes dust from the boards in the floor. He points.

"It's down here!" Jorge shouts.

The three of you pull up the boards to find three rotting human bodies beneath the floor.

"That's right," Mishil remembers. "Some Neolithic people kept their dead close."

"This is too close," Jorge whispers.

Worried about disturbing the grave, you replace the boards. When it's time to sleep that night, you and your friends are wide awake. It's impossible to sleep knowing there are dead bodies beneath you.

Turn the page.

The next morning, the three of you are exhausted. The villagers seem disappointed in the quality of your work. While learning to build a hut, you climb a ladder to smooth some mud onto an outer wall. It's becoming difficult to keep your eyes open. Without realizing it, you've fallen asleep.

You wake while falling from the ladder, landing with a smack against the hard ground. Finally, you can sleep. Forever.

THE END

To follow another path, turn to page 11.
To learn more about the New Stone Age, turn to page 103.

Pottery seems like the easier choice, but it's not. Before you get started, a woman with clay-caked hands leads you and Mishil to a muddy stretch of ground near the edge of the village. She hands you an adze and asks you to dig. You learn to separate the clay from the dirt.

In time, you and Mishil collect enough clay to make a few bowls. The woman slaps down a large mass of clay and shows you how to get started. It turns out you're a natural! Almost effortlessly, you form the clay into cups and bowls. Your work impresses the villagers.

You spend the rest of your days as a potter. You never do get back to the time you came from. Long after you die, one of your bowls ends up in the National Museum of Ancient Studies.

THE END

To follow another path, turn to page 11.
To learn more about the New Stone Age, turn to page 103.

You and Jorge decide to work with the animals while Mishil tries her hand at pottery. A man with long hair and a crooked smile teaches you how to feed them. Then he positions a deep clay pot beneath a cow and draws milk from the udder. You follow his lead.

As the sun sets, one of the villagers points to the woods and then to a nearby cow's skull. Jorge seems to understand.

"There are predators out there," he says.

Moments later, they hand you a spear and show you where to stand. They lead Jorge to another part of the village. Looks like you're on guard duty all by yourself!

It's not long before something approaches in the grass. You hear heavy panting and growling. It sounds like a pack of wolves or wild dogs.

Turn the page.

You stand with your spear ready, unsure what to do with it. Three large dogs approach slowly. They have big, sharp teeth. A dog from the village barks and runs to your side. You nod to the dog, and you swear he nods back.

"Let's do this," you whisper.

The dog barks again, and your heart thunders inside your chest. Having never used a spear before, you don't know how to attack. You could throw it and kill one of them to even the odds. Or you could hold your weapon to fight them off one at a time. Both choices make you nervous.

To throw your spear at the closest dog, go to the next page.

To hold onto your spear and jab at the dogs, turn to page 68.

You cock your arm and hurl the spear at the closest wild dog. In your gym class back home, you were pretty good at throwing a javelin. Unfortunately, throwing a spear at a moving target isn't the same thing. The dog runs toward you, and your only weapon sails over its head. You're defenseless as the dogs attack you.

You kick as hard as you can, but it's no use. The dogs knock you to the ground. The last thing you feel are piercing bites. Your New Stone Age adventure is over.

THE END

To follow another path, turn to page 11.
To learn more about the New Stone Age, turn to page 103.

You and your dog companion fight off the attacking beasts. You work together beautifully. You jab and stab at the wild dogs, while your dog fights them off with you. The beasts yelp in pain and scamper off into the woods.

The villagers have seen what you've done. The livestock has survived, and you're considered a hero. As a token of their gratitude, they present you with a fine knife, fashioned from a shiny, black stone. You show it to your friends.

"This looks familiar," you say excitedly.

"It looks exactly like the knife from the museum!" Jorge agrees.

"Do you think if we all touch it again we can get home?" Mishil asks.

"It can't hurt to try," Jorge replies. "I'm done with the New Stone Age."

"Okay," you say. "Let's give it a shot."

All three of you carefully touch the blade with your fingers. And just like that—you are back at the museum.

"There you three are," Mr. Hassan says. "Where did you wander off to?"

"Oh, just looking at some old stuff," Jorge replies.

You smile as you think about just how right he is.

THE END

To follow another path, turn to page 11.
To learn more about the New Stone Age, turn to page 103.

CHAPTER FOUR
NOMAD'S LAND

Thinking about becoming part of an ancient community is scary. Would the New Stone Agers accept you? And farming? Forget it. You don't know the first thing about raising crops.

"I say we take our chances on our own," you say.

Eventually everyone agrees.

"First things first," you say. "Let's find some food. I'm hungry!"

Jorge claps his hands once in excitement. "Let's build weapons and hunt down an animal—maybe a tasty boar. I could go for some pork chops."

Mishil shrugs. "Finding some fruit or nuts to eat will be so much easier," she says.

To hunt for food, turn the page.
To gather food, turn to page 73.

"Hunting seems smarter," you say. "Meat will give us more energy than nuts and berries."

"We'll need weapons," Jorge says.

You start making weapons for hunting. Mishil breaks sticks. You find a flexible branch to shape into a bow. Jorge has found some flat rocks. One has a sharp edge, perfect for sharpening sticks.

The three of you create a bow, some sharp sticks as arrows, and a few spears. Just as you finish carving notches into the arrow ends, Mishil speaks up.

"We should attach stone arrowheads to them," she says. "Like the ones in the museum displays."

The wooden arrows are probably pointed enough to pierce skin. Making arrowheads will take a lot more time, and your rumbling stomach doesn't want to wait any longer.

To try to make a handful of arrowheads, turn to page 74.
To use the sharp wooden arrows as they are, turn to page 77.

Mishil is right. Looking for food that can't run away or fight back seems like the best plan.

The three of you wander the plains, looking for something—anything—to eat. It's slow going trying to find edible plants or nuts in the great wide open. You finally come upon a cluster of bushes. Something bright catches your eye.

"Look," you say, pointing. "I found some berries we might be able to eat."

You examine the berries to decide whether they're edible or not. They are bright red and grow in tight clusters. More are growing on the surrounding bushes too.

"If we can eat these, they'll fill us up for a while," you say.

"What if they're poisonous?" Jorge asks.

To eat the berries, turn to page 87.
To find something else to eat, turn to page 93.

Even though your stomach growls, you decide to make arrowheads. What's the point in hunting with arrows that don't work? You search and find four small, flat rocks that could work.

Mishil explains how the ancient people sharpened the edges of the arrowheads. It takes a lot of effort to shape them to a point.

"It's getting pretty dark," Jorge says. "Let's set up camp and go hunting in the morning."

You and Mishil agree. The three of you camp beneath a stone outcropping in the hills. There you're protected from large wildlife. Mishil goes foraging in the woods for food and comes back with a handful of nuts. They're better than nothing.

The next morning you attach your arrowheads to the homemade arrows. They definitely look more deadly now.

Turn the page.

You, Jorge, and Mishil set off toward a wooded area. It's not long before you find a wild boar grunting around in the thick grass. You fire two arrows, and the second one hits. The boar squeals and runs across the plain.

"Hey!" Jorge shouts. "Our food is getting away!"

Mishil points to red drops on the grass. "Let's take our time and follow the blood," she suggests.

"If we don't hurry something else could get our boar," Jorge insists. "I'm sure it went this way." He points to a small cluster of trees down the hill.

You want to eat as soon as possible. Looking for the boar's trail would take some time, and there's no guarantee you'll find it. Jorge seems pretty sure he knows where it went.

To run after the boar before another predator gets it, turn to page 81.

To follow the trail of blood the boar left, turn to page 82.

The sharp sticks will work just fine. You want to eat as soon as possible. With spears, a bow, and a number of pointy arrows, you're ready to hunt.

Walking quietly through the trees, you spot a deer standing at the edge of a stream. You hook an arrow into the string and let the arrow fly. It bounces harmlessly off the side of the animal and it darts off.

"The arrows aren't sharp enough," Mishil says. "We need arrowheads."

"It might've just been an unlucky shot," Jorge says. "Maybe you didn't pull the bowstring back far enough?"

"We have to keep trying," you say as you grab another arrow.

The three of you wander around as dusk falls. At one point you see what looks like a large, dark bird and fire an arrow. It sails harmlessly past it.

Turn the page.

The three of you continue on, watching as the sun is just about to disappear behind the distant mountain range. As you listen for any more signs of animals, you hear a squishing noise to your left.

"Oh, gross," Jorge cries. "I stepped in something!"

The three of you quickly see that he's stepped in a mangled, rotting boar. It appears to have been torn apart by some sort of wild animal. Jorge's foot is covered in blood and guts.

"Did you hear that?" Mishil whispers.

It sounds like a growl from more than one creature. You ready an arrow and try to figure out where to aim as the last of the sunlight disappears from the sky. You see what looks like at least seven wild dogs walking through the grass toward you.

"They smell my bloody foot," Jorge cries.

Turn the page.

Before you can do a thing, the dogs rush the three of you. You let the arrow fly, and it bounces off the closest dog's head, doing no damage.

As you turn to run, you feel a dog sink its teeth into your leg. You never did get your dinner, but you've just become theirs.

THE END

To follow another path, turn to page 11.
To learn more about the New Stone Age, turn to page 103.

"Don't let it get away!" you shout, running.

The trampled grass in front of you is a good sign of where the boar is headed. Your classmates run behind you.

The boar's trail veers down a slope. The hill makes you run even faster. The wounded creature passes into a small cluster of trees, and you follow.

You break into the wooded area in time to see the boar dart through some of the trees. It slows down, and you lunge toward it.

The ground gives out beneath you. You're falling! It's a pit trap, set up by some hunters. Three sharp, spiky sticks pierce your body. As you bleed to death, you can hear your friends calling for you. You hope they don't meet your same fate.

THE END

To follow another path, turn to page 11.
To learn more about the New Stone Age, turn to page 103.

You decide to take your time and follow the blood instead of running headfirst into unfamiliar terrain. Finding blood spatters on the grass is tricky. As soon as your group reaches one, everyone looks for the next red spot. It helps to have three sets of eyes working together. Your heart sinks when it looks like you've lost the trail. You're about to give up and start over when Mishil shouts.

"I found it," she cries. "Over here!"

You and Jorge run down a hill. There, near a small cluster of berry bushes Mishil stands over your kill. The boar is lying on its side. It probably weighs 100 pounds. One of its tusks is sticking out of its mouth, but it isn't breathing or moving.

"It's dead," you whisper.

"What now?" Mishil says.

"Let's prepare it so we can cook it," Jorge says.

"We better skin it," you say.

Everyone works together to prepare your meal. You skin the boar and remove the hairy hide with a sharp stone. It's messy, bloody work. Mishil scrambles to build a fire. First she tries rubbing sticks together over a pile of kindling. When that doesn't work, she takes off her glasses and focuses the light of the sun on the pile of twigs and leaves. Soon she has a fire started. Jorge builds a spit with sticks to roast the boar.

After several hours, the fire roasts the boar nicely. The meal is delicious. You use as much of the animal as possible. Then you wrap up the leftovers in moist leaves. You'll need them in the days ahead.

Turn the page.

Weeks pass, and you and your friends get better at making tools and weapons. The three of you learn to live off the land. One day when you are out hunting in the woods, you spot a familiar knife. The tip of its blade is jammed into one of the trees. You stop and study it. Jorge and Mishil see you staring at the tree and come over.

"Hey," Jorge gasps. "That looks just like the knife we touched at the museum."

Mishil nods in disbelief. "I think it is," she whispers.

"Maybe if we all touch it at the same time . . ." you say.

"On the count of three," Jorge says.

"One, two," you say, and everyone touches the knife. There is a blinding flash. Suddenly you're back on the museum tour.

Turn the page.

"Three!" you say.

The students around you laugh.

"No, the Neolithic stage was longer than three years ago," the tour guide says with a smile. "Anyone else have a guess?"

Jorge and Mishil smile at you with relief. You've traveled into the past and back again but no one else seemed to notice. The rest of your class might be laughing at you, but it doesn't matter. You're home.

THE END

To follow another path, turn to page 11.
To learn more about the New Stone Age, turn to page 103.

You're unsure when you'll find something else to eat, and you're famished. Besides that, strawberries and raspberries are red, right? You try one of the berries. They're a little tart, but not half bad. Once your friends see you're OK, they try the berries too.

Before long, the three of you have eaten an entire bush full of berries.

"Well, that wasn't too bad," Jorge says. "I feel fine."

"Yes," Mishil says. "We might've gotten lucky. This could have turned out really bad."

You collect berries from the other bushes to eat later. As you do, you feel your stomach twist and your face suddenly feels really hot.

"Oh wow," Jorge says, touching his stomach. "Maybe we spoke too soon."

Turn the page.

Mishil's forehead is beading with sweat. She doesn't look good.

"These may have been poisonous after all," you whisper.

"Maybe we just ate too much," Mishil says, hopefully.

"We need to throw up," Jorge shouts. "To get this out of our systems!"

Your stomach is upset, but you're not convinced the berries were poisonous.

To try and throw up the berries, turn the page.
To wait for the sick feeling to pass, turn to page 92.

You hate the thought of throwing up, but death is definitely worse.

"We need to barf," you say to your friends, feeling your throat begin to tighten up slightly. You're not sure you can make yourself puke. Then Jorge helps you out by doing it first. That's all it takes. Both you and Mishil see this and immediately get sick. The three of you empty your stomachs. It's disgusting, but you do feel better.

"So, no berries," Mishil says, wiping the sweat from her forehead.

You're left feeling weak and unsettled. The three of you wander through the plains, hungry and miserable, but alive. As you forge ahead, looking for something to eat, you see familiar plants sticking up from the grass.

"That looks like wheat," Mishil says.

"I don't see how a few fistfuls of wheat will help," you say, "It's not like we have anything that can grind it into flour or any other way to actually eat it."

The four of you leave the wheat and wander for days. You struggle to find anything to eat. You find water but drinking it makes you sick to your stomach again. The hunger and weariness you feel leaves you wondering how nomadic people survived.

The last day that you are conscious, you see two deer dash by. Maybe you should have made weapons to hunt them when you were stronger. You're too weak to do anything anymore. You realize why New Stone Age people worked together and farmed.

You and your friends don't last long. Lost and hungry, the three of you starve to death.

THE END

To follow another path, turn to page 11.
To learn more about the New Stone Age, turn to page 103.

"We probably just ate too much," you say. "And if we throw up, we'll be hungry and dehydrated. Let's keep moving. I'm sure it will pass."

The three of you turn south, looking for water. You know that you can survive for a few weeks without food, but water is an absolute necessity.

Suddenly it feels like the world is starting to tilt a bit. Sweat soaks your forehead and neck. Your stomach gurgles and twists.

"I don't feel so great," Jorge mutters.

Your mouth feels dry, and your throat tightens. You're pretty tired. Mishil has fallen over and seems to be fast asleep. Jorge drops next. As you lose consciousness, you realize they're not sleeping. They're dead. Soon you are too.

THE END

To follow another path, turn to page 11.
To learn more about the New Stone Age, turn to page 103.

Eating a bunch of berries without knowing what they are seems dangerous. You have no idea if they're poisonous and decide it's not worth the risk.

"Let's leave the berries alone," you say.

"That's a good idea," Jorge says pointing to the ground. Lying nearby is a small, dead bird. "Did it eat these things?"

"Maybe," Mishil says. "Let's not test it out."

With wild berries off of the menu, it's time to move on. Your stomach growls. After some more walking, Mishil crouches down to examine a plant.

"Hey," she says. "I think this is wheat."

"Great," Jorge says, sarcastically. "Fistfuls of wheat. That sounds like a tasty meal."

Turn the page.

"New Stone Age people grew wheat in farms and in communities," Mishil says.

"We're nomads," Jorge reminds her. "We can't do anything with it. We need vegetables or fruits. Maybe some nuts."

You don't know what you'll do with the wheat, but it won't burden you to take some. You tear some animal skin from your clothes and make a crude pouch to carry it in.

"Maybe we'll find a prehistoric oven to bake bread in," Jorge says.

"Probably not," Mishil says.

As you venture on, you spot a small hut. Rows of crops grow nearby.

"Food," you whisper. "We could take some and finally eat."

Turn the page.

"If the farmers are friendly, maybe they'll give us some," Mishil suggests.

"What if they're not?" Jorge says. "Then we're still without food."

To sneak over to the farm and take some vegetables, go to the next page.

To approach the farm and talk to the people there, turn to page 98.

"We need to think of ourselves to survive," you say. "They'll never miss a few vegetables."

You all sneak through the high grass to the farm. It looks like they're growing peas and beans. You grab a handful of pea pods while the others pick beans. A dog barks at the edge of the farm.

"I forgot," Mishil says. "New Stone Agers domesticated animals. They have guard dogs!"

You panic as farmers approach. It's easy enough for them to tell what you're up to. Your heart races as the farmers surround you. Without a chance to explain how hungry you are, one of the farmers swings an adze at your head. The axe-like hand tool crushes the front of your skull. It's a nasty wound, and you die clutching a handful of stolen pea pods.

THE END

To follow another path, turn to page 11.
To learn more about the New Stone Age, turn to page 103.

You decide stealing isn't a great idea, even in the prehistoric past. The three of you approach the farm cautiously. A dog barks and immediately the six farmers there seem suspicious of you. You notice a few farmers hold spears, as if prepared to attack.

They speak a language you don't understand, so you point to your mouth and to your stomach, hoping to show you're all hungry. An older woman holds her hand out. You think she's asking for a trade. You open your pouch and hand her the wheat you've collected. She takes it and turns toward the farm.

"Hey," Jorge says. "She stole our wheat!"

"Maybe not," Mishil replies thoughtfully. "Just wait."

Turn the page.

Jorge relaxes. A few moments later, the woman waves you into the hut. She wants to pay for the wheat by feeding you a meal of grains and beans. It doesn't look very tasty, but you're too hungry to care.

Before you begin eating, you spot a familiar knife with a black stone blade sitting on the crude table.

"That looks just like the blade we touched that sent us here," you say. "Maybe it will send us home if we touch it again."

"You think it'll work?" Jorge asks.

"Only one way to find out," Mishil says.

The three of you place a finger on the stone blade at the same time. In a flash you are transported back to the museum. Mr. Hassan smiles as if you were never gone.

"I don't know about you three, but I'm glad the next stop is the cafeteria," he says. "I'm starving.

You look at your classmates and smile.

"We are too!" Jorge says.

THE END

To follow another path, turn to page 11.
To learn more about the New Stone Age, turn to page 103.

CHAPTER 5

ADVANCED ANCIENTS

Life in the New Stone Age, or Neolithic, changed the way ancient people lived. Roaming the wild, hunting and gathering food and finding temporary shelter was no longer the only way to live. Many people of the New Stone Age banded with others to build communities.

The Neolithic Revolution started sometime near 10,000 BC in the Fertile Crescent, a place located in the Middle East. People there started the first farms. Eventually farming spread to the rest of the world. On these farms, people built homes they could live in for long periods of time. Others built homes nearby creating villages of people willing to farm the land. As farms grew, so did the cities around them.

Working on the farms meant developing tools and useful items for survival. In addition to building weapons, people crafted instruments to till the land, pottery to hold water and food, and structures to contain their animals. Farming advancements during this time included irrigating fields and knowing how to grow different types of crops.

The ruins of Çatalhöyük in southern Turkey are all that remain of one of the largest Neolithic cities. Archaeologists have found shelters made of mud bricks. It's believed the site is at least 9,000 years old and as many as 8,000 people lived there at one time.

The Neolithic lasted close to 12,000 years. It was an important stepping stone toward modern-day human civilization.

TIMELINE

2.6 million years ago••

Stone Age
a time in history when humans made stone tools

2.6 million years ago••••••••••14,000 years ago
OLD STONE AGE
Paleolithic Period

14.000 years ago•••••11,000 years ago
MIDDLE STONE AGE
Mesolithic Period

1.7 MILLION YEARS AGO
Humans first made stone tools with sharp edges and symmetrical shapes.

40,000 YEARS AGO
First cave paintings appeared.

300,000 YEARS AGO
Hunters used tools and spears to hunt.

MESOLITHIC PERIOD
Hunters improved weapons. Humans built shelters near rivers and lakes. They gathered plants and stored them for future use. Pottery became more widespread.

•• 5,300 years ago

11,000 years ago••••••••••••••••••••••••••••••••••• 5,300 years ago
NEW STONE AGE
Neolithic Period

11,000 TO 10,000 YEARS AGO
Humans began farming instead of hunting and gathering.

9,400 YEARS AGO
Çatalhöyük, Turkey, was founded.

NEOLITHIC PERIOD
Humans began to use agriculture and build communities with permanent structures. They also domesticated animals for farming.

10,000 TO 8,000 YEARS AGO
Humans began to raise sheep, goats, pigs, and cattle for food.

OTHER PATHS TO EXPLORE

>>> Imagine that people during the New Stone Age never learned to farm and continued to hunt and gather. Do you think the human race would have lasted? Why or why not?

>>> New Stone Age people were the first to domesticate animals, including cows, sheep, and dogs. What do you think life would be like if humans had never tamed animals?

>>> The idea of farming first started in the Middle East, but in time spread all over the world. How do you think other humans discovered farming during this time?

READ MORE

Farndon, John. *The Rise of Civilization: First Cities and Empires.* Minneapolis: Hungry Tomato, 2018.

Hoena, Blake. *Could You Survive the Ice Age?* North Mankato, MN: Capstone Press, 2020.

Meyer, Susan. *The Neolithic Revolution.* New York: Rosen Publishing, 2016.

INTERNET SITES

First Farmers
www.dkfindout.com/us/history/stone-age/first-farmers/

How Did Stone Age Hunter-Gatherers Live?
www.bbc.com/bitesize/articles/z34djxs

Neolithic Facts for Kids
kids.kiddle.co/Neolithic

GLOSSARY

ceramic (suh-RA-mik)—having to do with objects made out of clay

conscious (KON-shuhss)—awake and able to think and perceive

dehydrated (dee-HY-dray-tuhd)—not having enough water

domesticate (duh-MESS-tuh-kate)—to tame something so that it can live with or be used by humans

harvest (HAR-vist)—to gather crops that are ripe; harvest can also be the crops that are gathered

irrigate (IHR-uh-gate)—to supply water for crops using channels or pipes

manure (muh-NOO-ur)—animal waste

nomad (NOH-mad)—a person who moves from place to place instead of living in one spot

predator (PRED-uh-tur)—an animal that hunts other animals for food

spit (SPIT)—a long, pointed rod that holds meat over a fire for cooking

BIBLIOGRAPHY

Hogenboom, Melissa, "Neolithic Farmers Used Manure on Crops," BBC News/Science and Environment, www.bbc.com/news/science-environment-23314510, Accessed June 19, 2019.

Newitz, Annalee, "How Farming Almost Destroyed Ancient Human Civilization," GIZMODO, io9.gizmodo.com/how-farming-almost-destroyed-human-civilization-1659734601, Accessed June 19, 2019.

Science Magazine Online
www.sciencemag.org/news/2015/08/archaeologists-uncover-neolithic-massacre-early-europe, Accessed June 19, 2019.

"This Stone Age Settlement Took Humanity's First Steps Toward City Life." *History Magazine*/Cities Issue. www.nationalgeographic.com/archaeology-and-history/magazine/2019/03-04/early-agricultural-settlement-catalhoyuk-turkey/, Accessed June 19, 2019.

INDEX